The Legend of
King Purplesnail

By

Jennifer K. Armstrong

Illustrated by Michelle Heiser

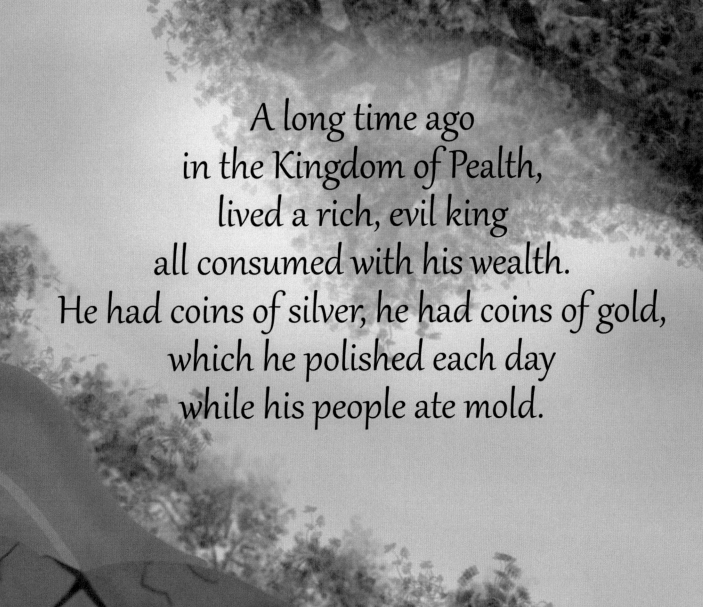

A long time ago
in the Kingdom of Pealth,
lived a rich, evil king
all consumed with his wealth.
He had coins of silver, he had coins of gold,
which he polished each day
while his people ate mold.

His greed was well known
throughout the whole land,
and his cruelty had gotten
way, way, out of hand.
He demanded his people
to give him more money,
and though they were poor,
he still found it funny.
"I'm wealthy," he'd say, "so what do I care
if my subjects are left
with not one pence to spare?"

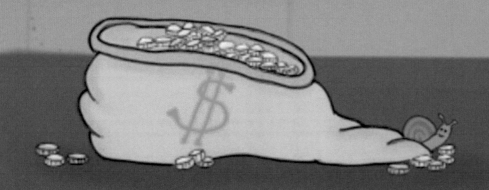

The people were angry, the people were mad.
They'd had kings before, but not one so bad.
"Let's storm the castle!"
someone said with a shout.
But soon everbody was filled with self-doubt.

For they were just peasants and the king was the king,
and no one had ever pulled off such a thing.
So there they stood, silent, all feeling quite weary
until a small voice said, "I have a theory."
Then everyone turned to see just who it was,
and lo and behold there stood little Buzz.

He was a young boy, and a small one at that.
He wore checkered pants and a
BIG floppy hat.
He looked rather puny, he looked rather weak.
But nobody stirred when he started to speak.

"The king is too tough to defeat in a fight,
so let's use our minds instead of our might."
The people were shocked, for Buzz was a kid.
They thought he was crazy, but listen they did.
"The king needs to see the mistakes he has made,
and for our hard work we deserve to be paid."

"We tend to his gardens, we care for his cows.
I even got stuck cleaning scum off his sows!
If we go on strike, then you know he will jail us,
and if we run off, then his soldiers will nail us."

"But if we can scare him and fill him with fright,
then maybe, just maybe, he'll do what is right."
And when he was finished, there was a slight pause,
then Buzz was engulfed in a roar of applause.

"But how will we do this?"
asked someone named Stan.

"The first step,"
said Buzz,
"is to make up
a plan."

And when they were done
and ready to go,
they started their plan
to get back their dough.

The following day while out for a stroll,
the king was approached by a menacing troll.

"Back off!" said the king,
"or I'll call for my knight!"

"If you wish," said the troll
"But we don't have to fight."

"If you let me go, then I'll tell you a tale
of the secret lost treasure of
King Purplesnail."

The king stopped short, "A treasure, you say?"

"Why, yes," said the troll, "and it's not far away.
King Purplesnail buried it deep in the ground,
and then drew a map so it could be found."

"Do you have the map?"
asked the king with much glee.

"I do," said the troll, "and it's yours for a fee."

"A fee?" said the king,
"But I already paid!"

"For the tale," said the troll,
"was the deal we made."

"So what is your price,
you miserable elf?"

"The price is you must dig it
up yourself."

"Dig for it myself?
I can't do such a thing!"

"You can if you try, you lazy old king."

The king thought for a moment,
but his greed was too big.
"Ok, I agree, now where do I dig?"

Out of his pocket the troll pulled a map.
And then to his head he gave a soft tap.
"Remember our deal, it is you who must dig.
The hole will be deep and the hole will be big."

"But when you are
through,
the dirt you will sift,
you'll hopefully find a
life-changing gift."

So the king took the map
and started his trip.
He went up a big hill and went down
a deep dip.

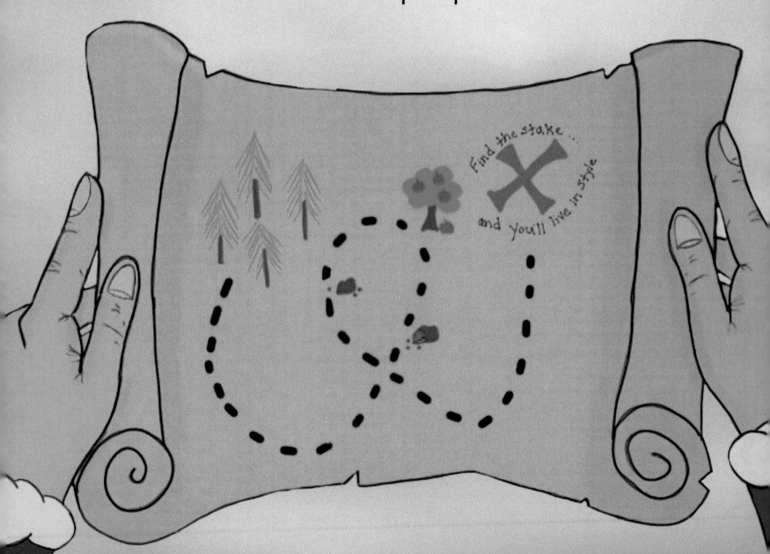

He went through the woods
and across a large field.
Then found a fresh apple and ate it unpeeled.
And while he was walking, he kept in his mind

an image of the wonderous
TREASURE he'd find.

But just when he thought that he'd made a mistake,
his foot tripped over
a small
wooden stake.

"It's just like the map,"
said the king with a smile.
"Find the stake,"
says the map,
"and you'll live in style."

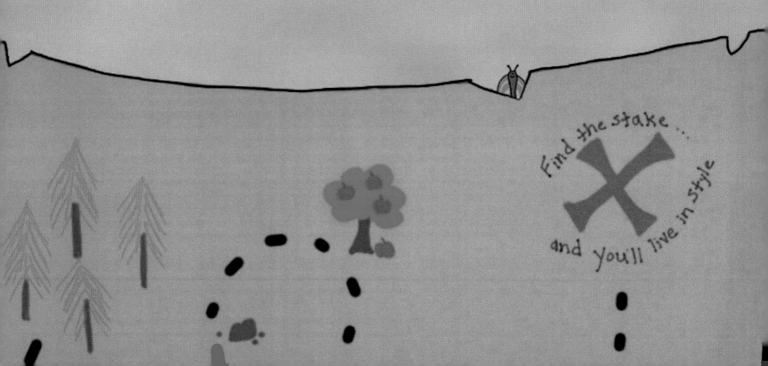

The king had no shovel, no tools which to use,
so, in desperation, he took off his shoes.
He scraped at the ground
with the left and the right,
he dug through the day
and he dug through the night.

And the more that he dug, the deeper he got,
but his greed kept him going
even though it was hot.
He kept up his digging, he felt like a mole.
Then all at once, found he was stuck in a hole.
"I've been tricked!" he exclaimed.
"That troll was a liar!"

And then a small voice said, "Listen here, Sire.
I may be a liar, but at least I'm not greedy.
You take from the poor
and you take from the needy.

So now it is you who is really in need
and none of your riches
can undo your deed."

The king squinted up at the top of the hole
and standing there, smiling, was the smart little troll.
"Oh, won't you please help me?" cried the pitiful king.
"I'm totally trapped and haven't a thing

to eat or to drink, not one little snack."
"Ok," said the troll, "if you give it all back."

"I will, oh, I will!" exclaimed the scared king.
"Now, PLEASE, won't you help me get
out of this thing!"
And so the small troll pulled the crying king out.
Then laughed when the king exclaimed
with a shout,

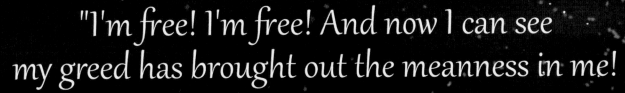

"I'm free! I'm free! And now I can see
my greed has brought out the meanness in me!

But evil no more—
from now on I'll
be fair, and so
with my people
my fortune I'll
share."

So, what is the moral
of this quaint little tale?
It is to be giving
and share without fail.
For if you are not,
you might meet a troll,
and dig yourself into
a very deep hole.

Made in the USA
Middletown, DE
12 October 2020